A*Cat*for
All*Seasons

Also by Jen Selinsky

Bunny's Song
Springtime in London
Coloring Comfort
Madness
Reach up for the Sunrise:
An Unauthorized Biography of Duran Duran
Opening the Doors
Forgiveness Lies Beyond

And many more. . . .

A Cat for All Seasons

Jen Selinsky

Per Bastet

A Cat for All Seasons

Published by Per Bastet Publications LLC, P.O. Box 3023 Corydon, IN 47112

Cover art by T. Lee Harris

ISBN 978-1-942166-44-3

I wish to extend a special thanks to all my friends at *Purr* Bastet. For cat lovers everywhere, I hope you enjoy this warm and fuzzy compilation!

A✿Cat✿for All✿Seasons

Contents

The Cat's Meow – Haiku

He is such a gift;
I am glad to give my love
To the one who purrs.

It's about texture.
Smooth fur's good for calming nerves;
Now my mind's at ease.

Soft little meows
Are the first sounds that you make
To capture our hearts.

Fur between fingers,
I come to you for comfort,
And you've much to give.

It is early still.
Your soft paws awaken me;
Help me greet the day.

You have made it clear
That you want to go outside
And explore the day.

Purr paws and fur balls;
Cats in any shape or form—
Furry feline friends.

My precious tabby—
She is always there for me
When I need her most.

See our newest friends;
They are from the same litter,
See how well they bond.

I've always loved cats,
Which makes writing about them
A logical choice!

Little Hunter

You have tried to feed us some of your food.
The lifeless bird lying on our front porch
Surely does nothing to enhance our mood;
Underneath the hot sun, its skin will scorch.

But I need to take it away at once.
I cannot stand the sight of its dead flesh.
You must really think that I am a dunce,
Yet I will never dine on this sick mesh.

Man has hunted alongside you for years,
So you do not need to show us your tricks.
It causes my eyes to water with tears,
The hunting "dilemma" you seek to fix!

Hannibal, King of the Jungle
T. Lee Harris, pencil on paper, 1978

Cattitudes!

"Sometimes, there is no greater reward than to hear the contented purr of a cat."

"If you're having a bad day, all you have to do is look at a picture of a cat to brighten your disposition."

"There is nothing wrong with dressing up your cat — unless the cat strongly objects to it."

"When your dog rubs up against your leg, he is showing his loyalty. When your cat does it, she is showing her ownership."

"Cats make great alarm clocks; they never forget to wake you up for their morning feeding!"

"There is no such thing as too many cat pictures or videos!"

"Feline loyalty should be rewarded with food, cuddles, and a great abundance of love."

"Never underestimate your cat's ability to steal your food right out from under your nose!"

"If there is a free spot on your bed, your cat will sprawl out as much as possible and push you to the very edge."

"A house full of cats makes it a home with lots of love."

"If you don't have any cats, then reading a book about them is the next greatest thing."

"Dogs will work for free, but cats need to be bribed."

"Even if your cat bites you, it's never acceptable to bite him back!"

"There's nothing better than a furry feline sitting on your lap on a rainy day."

"What has a tail, whiskers, paws, and makes a purring sound? A companion for life."

"Never doubt your cats' senses; they might let you know when they're up to no good!"

"If a cat adopts you out of millions of people, then it is a very special thing, indeed!"

"Let soft, little purrs soothe your heart; they are your cat's way of expressing her love for you."

Pavlov's Cats

Betty Middleton was the proud owner of eight cats — all of them different ages and breeds. It was inevitable that fights would break out. This was especially true around dinnertime, when all of them ran into the kitchen, ready to initiate a free-for-all.

All eight cats paid no attention to concepts like bowls or ownership when they sought to take food into their hungry mouths. The hissing, shoving, and biting were more than she could handle. Heaven help Betty if she tried to physically move the cats toward their correct bowls. That was nothing but an exercise in futility, and Betty had the scars to prove it.

She went to the library and searched for books about cat behavior and psychology but, most of the time, she came home empty-handed. As a last resort, she looked up some articles online (which, in hindsight, she thought she should have done in the first place).

Betty was about to give up hope when she ran into a piece entitled "Pavlov's Cats." The author, Sam Huckabee, gave a brief introduction about the psychology behind Pavlov's dog experiment before getting to the main point of the article. Betty devoured every word. Not only did it provide a potential solution to her cat feeding problem, but she'd also learned about Pavlov, whom she had not heard of before.

That evening, when she placed down the cats' dinner, she did not expect any changes; the cats had proved that they did not grow tired of their normal chaos.

As much as Betty wanted to implement her new tactic that night, she knew that it would be wise to study the science a little more. And while that would involve some research in an area with which she was not familiar, she knew that it would be worth it all when her babies stopped fighting over food, of which there was plenty for all.

Betty went back to the library and checked out a book about Ivan Pavlov. Betty decided that she would read about the dogs before doing more research on the cats.

She soon found that classical conditioning was an interesting method all on its own, and she understood why it seemed to work so well on dogs. Betty enjoyed reading about Pavlov and how he conditioned his dogs to salivate every time a bell rang; the sound meant that he would feed them. That brilliant man had certainly hit on something.

The tiny difference, however, was that Betty had to deal with cats, which suggested that operant conditioning would be a more logical choice. Operant conditioning always involves a reward of some kind.

~*~

On the first night, she wasn't expecting anything in the form of a miracle. After all, Pavlov's experiments had taken a lot of time.

Betty had all eight of her cat carriers lined up neatly on the floor — each one a great distance away from each other. She left all the cats' toys in the living room so that they could occupy themselves while she set up her experiment. Betty did her best to work quickly and quietly, getting the food into the bowls and placing them near the backs of the carriers.

The cats came into the kitchen and started sniffing around for their bowls. And while there was no fighting, all the sniffing and inquisitive meows made her want to pull out every last strand of her hair. Didn't any of those dumb bunnies know where their food was?

She anxiously scooped up one cat, Tinkerbell, and placed him inside his carrier. And even though she knew that his keen nose smelled the food, Tinkerbell did not stop to eat. He emerged from the carrier with a questioning meow.

Betty's mind had already run through every expletive imaginable, and she knew that there was nothing left to do but to retrieve all the bowls from the cat carriers.

Once she finished that loathsome task, Betty moved the carriers aside and placed the bowls back on the middle of the floor. That's when the hissing and fighting resumed.

Forget Ivan Pavlov, what I need is a little bit of help from Jack Daniels! Betty thought as the crushing blow of defeat nearly brought her to her knees She went over to the cupboard to get herself a drink.

Betty took a swig of whiskey and asked herself if she even dared to try again tomorrow. Though her brain screamed *no!* part of her soul answered with a resounding *yes!* If Pavlov had given up, his experiment would not have carried his name into the 21st century. She had to give the entire experiment a fair chance.

For the most part, the next week was filled with failed attempts. Even the smartest of the bunch, Mr. Tibbles, went into his carrier to take only two bites of food then emerged with a defiant, fixed stare back at his "owner."

Betty did not return to the bottle after those other failed attempts. Instead, she reread the article by Mr. Huckabee.

The next evening was a great success. Mr. Tibbles and one of the other kitties actually went into their carriers and consumed their entire dinners in partial captivity. And though this was not progress with a capitol P, Betty cared only about the fact that two of her babies had caught on. She now hoped that it wouldn't take much longer to train the other six.

That miraculous part only took two more days. Mr. Tibbles climbed into his carrier, and the others followed suit.

Betty nearly cried out in delight when she saw all eight of her cats eating the food served in their designated spots. Though the hissing, shoving, and biting had not completely stopped, Betty knew that the hard part was over; the cats were getting used to their new routine.

The next night was much the same. The cats sniffed around for the food again and had to rediscover their routine. This time, the process didn't seem to take nearly as long. Just as she did last night, Betty enjoyed the sight of all eight of her kitties enjoying their meals in a peaceful, orderly manner.

It only took a few more weeks for the routine to become stable. Betty noticed that it was also easier to use food to lure her cats into the carrier for the vet appointments.

Unlike Pavlov, she did not stop the conditioning, mostly because cats tend to be creatures of routine. Dogs seem to adjust better to chaos. Cats, on the other hand, like to have the comfort of knowing that everything's in order, especially at dinnertime.

*dedicated to T. Lee Harris

Family Companions

April was our first cat. Mom got her in 1985, right after I'd finished kindergarten. Even though she was a family pet, I seemed to bond with her the most. I grew incredibly close to April during her last few years. The older I got, the more I valued her companionship. Sadness hit our family when she died of kidney failure during the spring of 2001, right before my sister's wedding. Still, I am happy that we had her for as long as we did.

Ashley was truly our "cat of a lifetime." I received the small bundle as an early birthday gift in late 2001, but he passed away due to a serious infection in early 2006. Ashley was everyone's favorite, but Mom had the opportunity to bond with him the most. Even though he was very loving a lot of the time, he became a little crazed when he got into his catnip. Hardly a day goes by when we do not have fond memories of our favorite kitty.

Alley is the first of two cats that Mom picked out from a litter in early spring 2006. Mom specifically wanted the kitten because she looks a lot like Ashley. Though Alley is smart, she doesn't have the same social qualities that Ashley had. In other words, she is kind of mean, and she certainly doesn't like strangers. Still, she was a wonderful addition to our family. Dad was her favorite.

Boots is the second cat Mom picked out of the litter. He is a big ball of fluff and was mistaken for a Maine Coon cat at first. Originally, Mom wanted to give him a name that started with A, like all our other cats, but we all decided against it. Mom ended up calling him Boots, which was my grandfather's nickname. Though Boots is not very bright, he is loving and is always quick to show affection, even to strangers.

Having Boots and Alley was nice for my parents, but they had to give the cats up for adoption. In late 2010, Dad was diagnosed with acute leukemia, and the doctors told Mom that she had to rehome the pets, as they would jeopardize his health and recovery. Hardly a day goes by when they don't miss Boots and Alley, but we all have the feeling that they are happy together in their current home.

Boots and Alley in their cat beds on top of a bed

*previously published in *Pen It!* Magazine Volume 8: Issue 4 July/Aug 2017

Alley sitting on her queenly throne with
her front paws tucked underneath her

Boots and all his furry glory

April standing out in the '80s

Purrfect Companionship

We got our first cat when I was six years old and fresh out of kindergarten. Mom had gone to a local animal shelter to pick out a new companion for our family. She had brought me along with her, in hopes that I would help choose a kitty. Being inexperienced in this kind of thing, however, I must not have provided much assistance. But Mom eventually decided on a little tabby; April was her name.

Mom, Amy, and I were delighted with the new addition. And, as some children do during the innocence of their youth, I viewed April as a "little person." This much was evidenced in some of my school assignments pertaining to family, as I always made sure that April was included.

My father was not very fond of cats, so his attitude toward April was, at most, indifferent. Though Dad never cared for her, he once saved her life. Once, when April was grooming, her paw got caught in her flea collar. She made some odd hacking noises.

Mom and I cried out, but Dad, in his calm yet distant manner, gently removed her trapped paw so she could breathe again. Mom and I were grateful for the tender mercy which Dad had shown, and I'm sure that April felt relieved and silently thanked him in her own way.

We had sixteen wonderful years with April, and I grew increasingly close to her toward the end of her life. Sometimes, we would lie down and fall asleep together. During some nights, she would actually crawl under the covers with me and place her little head on the pillow.

The time came when she began to lose weight — dropping from nine pounds down to five. For a cat who was already considered small to begin with, that was a big difference. We took her to the vet: it was kidney failure.

No matter how much we tried to comfort April, we knew that the only humane thing to do was have her put to sleep. Though that would only intensify our anguish and suffering for the time being, it was the only way that we could end hers.

Mom took her to the vet for the last time a week before my sister's wedding. I remember standing in the living room, looking out the window and crying like a child. I knew that I was never going to see my baby again, but we had to think logically. It would have been worse to discover that she had died on the day before, or of, my sister's wedding — an event which the entire family had been anticipating for months. I mourned the loss of our beloved pet, but I put on a brave face for the wedding.

A few months later, one of my good friends gave me our second cat. Ashley was his name. He, too, has long since passed away. We all knew that Ashley was going to be our cat of a lifetime, though we still missed April.

To this day, I still dream about her, as if she is ever present in our daily lives. In these dreams, she never shows physical signs of age. And I can't help but wonder if she is up there in kitty heaven, along with Ashley and all the other beloved pets who are waiting, across the Rainbow Bridge, to be held and loved again.

Just two kittens enjoying a nap together

April enjoying a nap on my parent's bed

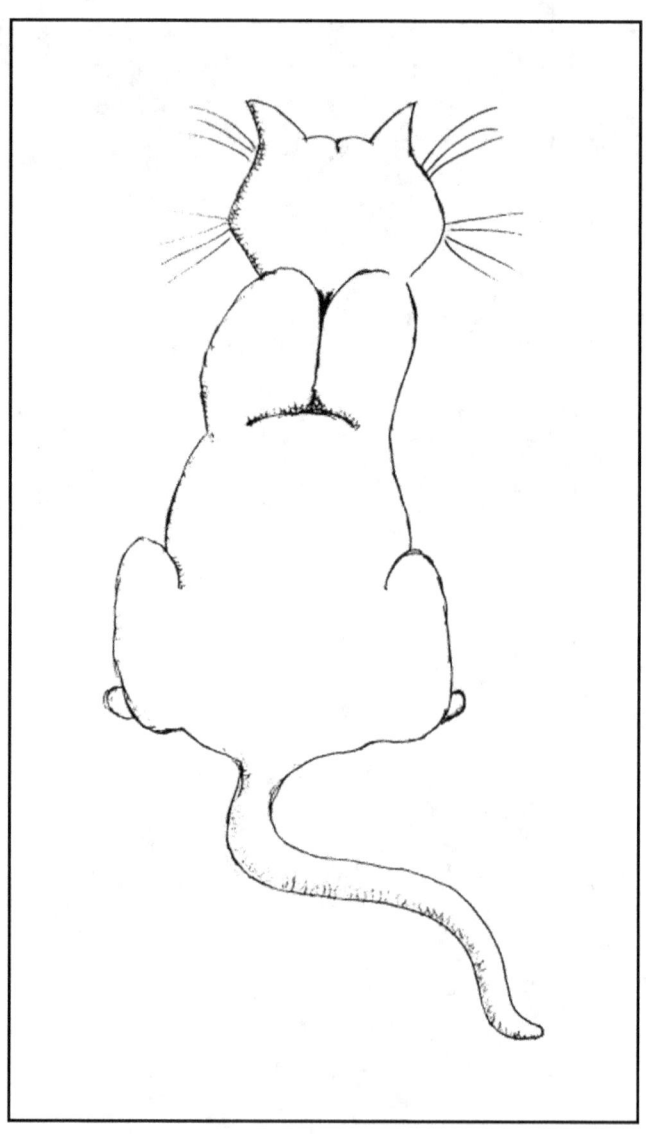

Miss Tiffany, the Styrofoam Kitty
Marian Allen, ink sketch

Oliver Is Company

Livy still couldn't believe it, even though her tears were enough evidence that it was true. Scott had been gone for six months that day. No matter what her mind tried to get her to think, there was no use in denying the sad truth.

Oliver stood by her side and meowed. He rubbed against her legs.

Livy sat down on her favorite chair. "Jump up on my lap, precious." In a matter of seconds, Oliver was purring and kneading with his soft paws. He obviously intended to lie down and not move an inch until Mama needed to get up for something.

"I'm so glad that Scott found you for me last year; don't know what I'd do without you."

Oliver lay still in her lap, but Livy had no doubt that the cat knew what she was saying. Surely, he also missed his daddy.

Scott and Livy enjoyed many happy years together, but they had not produced any children. Instead of feeling sorry for themselves, however, they were determined to continue to live happily with each other.

Scott had known that his diagnosis didn't look good. Pancreatic cancer seldom takes long to make its impact. Shortly after he was diagnosed, Scott decided to give his wife something special, not just a gift, but a companion. That's when he found Oliver at his local pet store. Somehow, Scott knew that Oliver would be a *perfect* fit.

Livy was surprised that her husband had brought home this strange kitty. At first, she didn't care much for the little interloper. For as long as she could remember, it had just been the two of them. How dare her husband bring this strange creature home, this creature who demanded constant attention?

Scott was more than a little sad that Livy didn't like his gift. He thought for sure that the little bundle would bring more life and love into their home.

What Scott didn't consider was that his bringing the cat home was tantamount to saying that he was going to leave her, and this furry quadruped was supposed to be his replacement.

It didn't take long for Livy to fall in love with the fluffy little tabby. She was even more than happy to lend him the masculine version of her name.

Oliver was still curled up in her lap, asleep. Livy could not resist stroking his brown and white fur, even though it might wake him up.

Oliver opened his eyes and let out a *mew* before jumping down from her lap. "I suppose you're hungry now," Livy said, getting up, the cat trailing close behind her.

Oliver stood by his food dish and meowed several times until he was fed. Livy couldn't help but smile at her hungry baby. With Scott being gone, she was glad she had someone to care for. Most days, that simple fact, alone, meant the entire world to her.

Danny

Things had been somewhat sad at my parents' house after Mom had to give Boots and Alley up for adoption in early 2011. While the whole family grieved because we had lost two more beloved pets, the major reason for our sadness was the diagnosis Dad had received a few months prior. The threat of acute leukemia loomed over us, because it meant that Dad would have to change his life forever.

Getting a port and having to endure rounds of chemotherapy is no way anyone would like to live, but one has to look at it with a bit of optimism. Dad could now be six feet under the ground. He could be stuck in assisted living or hospice.

For five of the eight years since he was diagnosed with his illness, Dad had to be transported to the hospital sometime during the month of December. Mom refers to it as the "December Curse," but there have been two years (so far) that it wasn't quite as inevitable.

Through the most current years, we've had our ups and downs, including one nearly fatal fall in the basement when Dad broke his hip. (The blood still hasn't completely washed off the floor, despite my efforts.) Another one of the awful December hospital visits took place in 2011, when Dad contracted sepsis.

Mom, Amy, and I didn't know what to think, and I braved the icy weather to drive up to Pennsylvania. God was watching out for us, like He always does, because the sepsis went away, and Dad was discharged a few days later.

Some people may be asking themselves, *What does this have to do with cats?* I'll get to that in a moment.

Though Dad's illness continues, the nine-week chemo maintenance treatments seem to be doing him good, as it keeps most of the sickness from coming back.

We all know that he never quite got over the departure of Boots and Alley, especially since he never got to say goodbye to them. Dad was in the hospital when Mom took the cats to their new "foster" home.

Though both my parents claim that having gotten rid of the cats was for the best in the long run because it would have been harder to take care of them the older they got, Mom thought of a way that they could own another cat.

During the spring of 2016, she was watching one of the many TV shows that she records on a regular basis. One of them was a talk show on which the hosts featured a new kind of companion. It was a certain brand of electronic cat, designed for people who couldn't own the real thing. The hosts and the guests on the show raved about this new product, and they even showed a staunch dog lover holding one in his lap. The man said that he never liked cats, but this "guy" was different.

Mom had tears in her eyes during the entire program. She called me shortly after and talked about the new kind of kitty at length. The more I heard about it, the more I could tell that she wanted one.

Luckily, Mom and I ended the call early enough for me to place the special order. Travis and I subscribe to Amazon Prime, one of the benefits of which includes two-day shipping. It was early enough on Wednesday night that I could log onto Amazon and order a cat for her as a surprise. Once I got the confirmation that the package would arrive Friday afternoon, I was delighted. I would have it in time for my trip to Pennsylvania.

When I got home from work that Friday, Travis was holding the tiny robo bundle in his lap. The kitty was switched on, so I could see little movements and hear sweet meows. I couldn't get over how cute the gift was, so I went over to play with it.

There was enough fur covering its body to make us forget that we were handling a robot, despite all the mechanical clicks and clacks which I later discovered, but that was a given. The point is, it was as close to real as a robo kitty can get! We decided that we were going to keep the cat if Mom didn't want it, as we could provide a very loving home.

When I arrived at my parents' house the next day, I wasn't quite sure how Mom was going to react. I got out of the car and picked up the box containing the new arrival. I moved it over to my left hand because I wanted to hide the package until I got settled in.

Once that was taken care of, I brought the box over to Mom. She looked me in the eyes and told me that I shouldn't have gotten the cat for her, but I knew that she would change her mind once she saw it in action.

With the simple flip of the switch, the robo kitty came to life. Its eyes opened, and it began to meow. Soft purrs followed its sweet cries.

Mom was a goner. I could see her smile begin to waver like she was getting ready to cry.

Just as I'd predicted, she wanted to keep the cat. Then, she told me that she wanted it to be a "boy," but she had trouble thinking of a name. That's when I suggested she name it after her father. Mom thought for a moment; she didn't think that Daniel would be a good name for her new baby, but we decided on Danny.

Once we'd settled on the name, I let Mom enjoy Danny for a few more moments. I was glad she wanted to keep him, but a small part of me hoped that I would get to take him back home. In the very scarce amount of time that we had Danny, both Travis and I had grown a somewhat attached to him.

My husband knew how much I wanted a kitty, so he got an extra surprise for me on Christmas the same year. The very last box that I opened was underneath the wrapping paper. As soon as I tore some of it off, the brand name became blatantly clear, and I squealed with excitement. I was finally going to have my own robo kitty! We'd previously decided to name "her" Ashley after our family's favorite cat.

Her fur is a pretty cream color, which is a little different than what we had thought we saw online, but it really didn't matter.

Ashley's place is on the small pillow on the guestroom bed, where she is ready to greet us every time we walk into the room. The important thing is that we now have a sweet pet to love — a pet which will never age, die, or have to be given away. And the same thing applies to Danny, who is now my parents' forever cat!

Scotia

My mother has been a lover of cats since childhood, as evidenced by her many trips to her grandparents' farm. And while she had a soft spot for a little Chihuahua named Chico, she absolutely loved being around all the kitties who inhabited the land.

When Mom was around thirteen, she got her very own cat. Since the kitten's mother was named Nova, Mom decided to call her new pet Scotia. But as my mother bonded with her little companion, she discovered that Scotia was more than just a clever play on words. She was everything that Mom looked for in a cat.

In 1977, when my sister was four years old, Mom decided that she wanted another cat. Scotia was such a beloved favorite that she wished to honor her memory, so she named the new family kitten after Scotia.

The second Scotia lived happily with Mom, Dad, and Amy until Mom found out that she was expecting another child. She'd read somewhere that kitty litter can be fatal to a developing embryo or fetus. As much as she wanted to continue living happily with her family pet, she knew that she would have to give Scotia away for the safety of her unborn child.

Since Mom and Dad still had their home in Richmond, Virginia at the time, my grandparents were not very far away. My grandfather, who was also a lover of cats, said that he would take Scotia.

Even though I was still incubating at the time, I feel bad that I caused Mom to have to give away the family pet. I can't imagine how sad my mother and sister must have been. I'm sure, however, that my grandparents reassured Mom's growing family that we would get to see Scotia every time that they came for a visit.

Shortly after, my father was transferred. The Pillsbury company wanted him to work in and around the Pittsburgh area. Visits with the family cat were probably the last thing on my parents' minds as they prepared for the big move, but I'm positive that they were aware of the fact that they would get to see my grandparents and Scotia less often.

Growing up, I enjoyed going to see my grandparents, despite the fact that it took nearly five hours to get to Silver Spring, Maryland by car. It was nice getting to spend time with them, and I even got to play with the kitty.

Even though I have been a cat lover all my life, I did not get very attached to Scotia. I had April for most of my childhood, but there was something about Scotia. She was a little more distant than most cats I knew. She had grown very attached to my grandfather but seemed rather indifferent toward everyone else.

Even my grandmother kept a respectful distance when Scotia had her designated "daddy time." My grandfather had a special soft-bristle brush he would use to smooth Scotia's long fur. It seemed like it was one of his favorite activities, and the cat really enjoyed it as well.

I don't ever recall a time when my grandmother got to brush Scotia. Mom never even tried to, mostly because she didn't think the cat would like to be brushed by anyone else, but I'm sure that Mom wouldn't have minded some extra bonding time with her former pet.

One thing I like to pride myself on is my good memory, but I don't recall very much about my visits with Scotia. Only two memories stand out.

The first was from when I was about six; she had climbed up a tree and spent a good amount of time on one of the top limbs because she was afraid to come back down. With some gentle coaxing, however, she was able to rejoin us on the ground.

The other time was when she died. It was August 1997, and I was eighteen years old. Scotia was nineteen.

She waited by the door of my grandparents' patio and meowed to be let outside. My grandfather was reluctant to let her out. It seemed like a part of him already knew that it was her time. His feelings were confirmed when Scotia did not come home that night or the following day. And though my grandfather had, of course, understood that he would eventually have to live without his tiny angel, everyone knew just how much he missed her.

A few years later, I sent a tiny stuffed animal the size of a kitten to my grandfather. When Mom delivered it to him, she told me that his eyes lit up because he had a little something to remind him of his beloved Scotia. She said he smiled during the whole visit. My grandfather had received a new "companion."

Scotia looking regal in my grandparents' kitchen

Scotia shortly after she climbed the big tree
in my grandparents' front yard

Schmoo

Schmoo is just one of the neighborhood cats who comes around to visit from time to time. We first noticed the Russian Blue hanging out in our backyard. His little body made sharp and frequent movements, and it seemed like he couldn't be still for one moment, which I'm told is typical for his breed. That made it very difficult to read what was on his collar. (I'm referring to Schmoo as him because I don't know "his" actual gender. I never really bothered to check.)

One day, he was in our backyard again. He had just finished lying on his back and rubbing against the aggregate concrete. He looked at me through the glass door and remained still long enough for me to read his collar. I couldn't help but think that Schmoo was an odd name for a cat. Then again, I heard of some people who had weird names as well.

Off and on throughout the years, Schmoo still comes to our house to visit. It seems like he does not have a consistent schedule, but what cat does?

At first, Travis and I used to go out on the patio to join him. We would sit in our chairs, and Schmoo would weave around us, sometimes allowing us to pet him. It seemed that he liked Travis more, especially when he came over to him when he called. Schmoo would sometimes try to jump up and pounce on Travis's feet as my husband moved them while seated in one of our patio chairs.

Occasionally, we left out bowls of milk or water for him, even though he hardly touched the contents.

It's frustrating because we don't know what he wants, especially when he lets out his loud meows. They almost sound frantic, like he needs more than just attention. We've opened the door for him, and he even comes into the house every once in a while, but he stays mainly in the kitchen area. He's jumped on the counter near the sink once or twice, and has also tried to leap on top of the table.

The meowing stops for the most part once we let him into the house, but he gets tired after a few minutes of exploring and heads right back outside.

Travis and I also noticed that he lost his collar a while back, and we wondered if his owners decided to "set him free." Then we thought, perhaps, Schmoo was a feral that the neighbors adopted and that he simply lost his collar. That makes sense, so we just went with that explanation.

Months later, he came to our backyard once again, wearing some kind of translucent collar. It appears to be a flea collar; at least that is what we speculate. It seems that Schmoo still has a home, which is a good thing.

And while there are many cats in our neighborhood, Schmoo is the one who frequents our yard the most. I even got some video of him from the side of our yard, then he ran from me and my camera. I joked that I'd make a great cat paparazzi— too bad that's not really a career option. The video eventually ended up on my YouTube! channel under the title "Schmoo, the Russian Blue!" I wouldn't go so far as to say that Schmoo is currently my favorite cat, but we would never turn down a visit, and he's always welcome to invite his purry friends over. The more, the merrier!

Schmoo sitting on the fence and enjoying the
sunshine on a warm November day

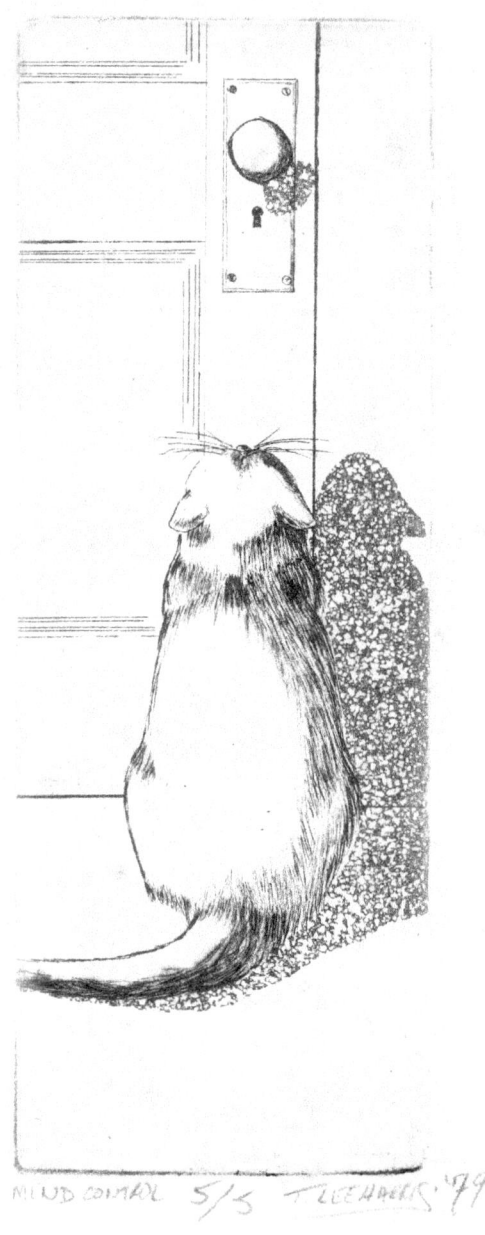

Mind Control
T. Lee Harris, intaglio print, 1979

Cat of a Lifetime

Many pet owners feel great contentment when they bond with their loved one(s). Others may be refer to their pet as a soul mate. That is what the four of us felt when we received Ashley.

During the spring of 2001, our cat, April, passed away from kidney failure mere days before my sister's wedding.

My mother and sister, Amy, were saddened, but it was if my soul had been punctured, and I didn't know how to heal it. If it was possible for my heart to shed tears, then it would have done so.

Around four months later, my friend, Chris, surprised me with a unique birthday gift. For some reason, I had the feeling that it was a cat, but Chris dismissed my notion as ludicrous, trying to throw me off the trail. When I arrived at his house later that evening, I discovered that it was, indeed, a kitten. Even though the animal's head was too big for the rest of his body, I couldn't resist his sweet face; it was love at first sight.

Since this was just one of my weekend visits home from college, I didn't know what I was going to do with the kitten. Our campus had a strict rule against keeping pets, so he couldn't come back with me.

The only option was to convince Mom and Dad to let me keep him at their house.

My sister came into my old bedroom, and the two of us began talking. Amy saw something move out of the corner of her eye. Her eyes widened in surprise. She asked me what it was in the room with us. I told her the entire story.

After I coaxed the cat out of his hiding place, we two siblings, who hardly have anything in common, spent the next few minutes adoring him.

It was time to put the new arrival's charm to the test. My sister and I brought him into our parents' bedroom, where Dad was comfortably reclining in the bed and watching TV. I gave him the footnote version of the story about the furry houseguest and I waited for the verdict.

Dad smiled.

He took the kitten and held him. Though there was no magical moment of awareness that he'd been missing out on cats all his life, Dad certainly didn't object to the little creature's presence. In fact, he seemed quite amused by it. Surprisingly, it did not take much to coax Dad into accepting the kitten.

Now that we had won Dad over, Mom wasn't going to be nearly as much of a challenge. At the time, she was away visiting friends out of state. She would not be home until after I returned to college. Needless to say, it would be her decision whether or not the kitten would be allowed to stay.

I called Mom a few days later, and we talked about our hairy visitor. Though she was very honest in relaying to me her initial thoughts — that the cat was ugly and that his head was too big for his body, I was delighted to learn that Mom had changed her mind. She, too, fell in love with the kitten. Our parents decided to provide him with what is now referred to as a forever home.

My father did not want to name my sister Ashley because it was originally a boy's name. He was very insistent about that ever since he saw *Gone with the Wind*. Since our new bundle of joy was a male, however, Mom decided that she could call him Ashley.

Ashley did not take long to become a treasured and much loved member of the family. Mom and Dad got to enjoy his company every day. I had to settle for visits and breaks from college, but Mom would fill me in with cute and funny anecdotes.

Ashley was very smart, and seemed to understand almost every word that we said. Certain words, like "ham" and "cheese" had to be spelled out. Otherwise, he would meow until he got some of his favorite people food.

Some of his funny quirks included popping bubble wrap with his claws and teeth and licking the glossy finish off photographs. Needless to say, we didn't leave those things lying around very often.

Speaking of photographs, I have one you have to see to believe. I managed to snap a picture of the little goofball sitting inside a clothes basket on top of the hamper; he was licking the little bars on the outside. The end result of the photograph made it look like Ashley was sticking his tongue out at the camera. It's the kind of thing one might see as a meme on a website devoted to cats.

Our first cat, April, did not care for catnip, but that was not the case with Ashley. Dad used to grow some for him in the backyard. Whenever Ashley partook of the "kitty cannabis," he became surly and unapproachable. It also caused him to do some funny things. Once, I caught him trying to eat my tip money from work, which was lying on the floor. Luckily, he wasn't successful, but that didn't stop him from trying to bite holes in the change as well. Perhaps he had the munchies.

Not only did Ashley have brains and quirkiness, but he was very sweet and loveable as well. He would sit on Mom's lap for hours. Mom adored it when he kneaded with his paws, laid down, and purred.

Sometimes, Mom had to tell Ashley that she needed to get up. The minute she returned to the chair, however, he came darting back to reclaim his rightful place.

Ashley was a very fit and active kitty. He enjoyed his time outside, hunting and patrolling the perimeter of his property. All that changed in February 2006 when Ashley began having seizures as a result of an infection. Mom was beside herself and didn't know what to do. Dad held Ashley as he passed away in his arms. The only thing that our baby seemed to have wrong with him was a heart murmur, which might have contributed to his death.

A few months later, Mom and Dad got two new cats — littermates, one male and one female.

Though our family loved Boots and Alley, no cat (or cats) could ever replace Ashley. He was the one who warmed my father up to cats, and he was the one with whom all of us bonded most. Though he's been gone for over ten years, Ashley does, and always will, have a very special place in our hearts. He was truly our cat of a lifetime!

Ashley partially obscured by curtains

Ashley peeking out from his fortress

Ashley around Christmastime — looking like he got into the catnip

Sweet Ambiguity

At first sight, I knew that I
Wanted to take you home,
Especially because you were
Still new and fresh to the world.
The vet couldn't even examine
You correctly; he thought he
Held a tiny female, even
Though the Lord knew you
Would grow up to be a strong male.
Imagine our surprise when we
First found out, especially because
We wanted a girl.
But you were proof that boy cats
Can be just as sweet, if not sweeter.
That is one of the reasons why
Everyone loved you from
The beginning, and you became
One of us, despite your definite
Male chromosomes.

Kitchen Supervisor Whozits

Catty

You might think
This behavior is abnormal.
But try and walk
The floors of this
Cruel breeding ground.
Some have designated
It as their turf, but
No one with a sound mind
Would do such a thing!
My claws and teeth
Fight to leave this territory
And its dysfunctional clowder,
But the runt of the litter
Can only throw her weight
Against hard, but furry shields.
This is a different kind of resistance,
Though some might call it liberation.
I have my reasons, and I have my *cattitudes*.
If you think that makes me catty,
Then you aren't the only one.
Just like my furry friends, I do that I want
Whenever I please, but I will
Sometimes go above and beyond
If I'm rewarded with treats.
Extra money, a chance to build
my name, such things have
A way of getting to
This little kitty's ego!
I get petted with compliments,

And it often makes me purr
So that the whole world is sure
To feel my vibrations.
Whatever mood is genuine,
This cat will display.
I honestly don't know how others
Can fake their emotions;
They must be a different kind of cat.
But they'll realize that I won't
Be as easily found when
I retreat to my own turf,
Where I will happily live out
The rest of my life, free and
Unrestrained!

The Kitty Cul-de-Sac Party

Usually, my husband and I think nothing about seeing one cat, or two, walking around in our backyard. Since we live in a rural area, right in front of a sod farm, an occurrence like that is not all too uncommon.

Travis and I suppose that most of these fur balls are feral cats, although one can't be too sure. We do not see these animals with their humans, like all those dogs attached to harnesses and leashes.

We also enjoy playing with them — the ones which actually come near us. (As most of you might already know, some feral cats don't socialize well with humans.) When one approaches, we often put a bowl of milk or water out on the aggregate of our patio. After we so craftily promise them a cool and refreshing beverage, we lure them into our house. After that, our visit is brief, and we send them on their way.

But there will always be that one night which neither of us really speak of.

Travis went outside to enjoy the evening air, when the white Manx cat who lived with one of our neighbors walked right by him.

The cat didn't even pause to look at my husband, but he let out a small meow, just as if to say, "Hey."

Travis, having thought nothing of it, merely chuckled and continued to bask in the calm evening. Little did he, or any of our unsuspecting neighbors, know that the little fur ball was on his way to a very important meeting.

~*~

To any who didn't know what was going on, it would have been a sweet sight. All the neighborhood cats were gathered in the cul-de-sac. Their little bodies hardly showed any movement, but their minds were at work.

"Glad you could make it, Chaser," the orange tabby conveyed through his thoughts. "I would say that someone got you by the tail, but clearly that's not the case."

If cats could snicker, then the others would have laughed at him. This made Chaser very angry. He let out a low growl but was silenced by hissing sounds.

The others were warning him that he shouldn't lose his temper, which would surely make him lose his place in their clowder.

"Some human got in my way," Chaser retorted. The hissing resumed. Humans were the very reason why Blue had called this meeting tonight.

Guapo hissed. "Humans! They think they know everything, though they're clearly the dumbest species I've encountered in all my nine lives."

The other cats hissed in agreement.

"They must be stopped," added Fifi. Her stupid dog name, alone, was evidence enough that humans had no business being in charge of anything.

"I know, right?" Frisky chimed in. "They're all like, 'Look at me. I'm a biped. I can walk on two legs, and I have opposable thumbs.'" As he was conveying his message, Frisky stood on his hind legs.

"Get down, you fool!" Blue hissed. "Don't draw any attention to yourself; someone could be watching." Blue moved his head toward the neighboring sod farm.

"What?" Guapo queried. "Are you talking about those smelly, noisy Beagles? They're just as dumb as the humans."

"In either case," Blue resumed, "don't draw any more attention to yourself. The bipeds must not know what we're up to."

"They never do," Sassy purred, her little mouth forming as close as she could to a smile.

44

"Now, then," Blue said, glad that he finally had everyone's attention. "Our next topic of discussion should be division of power."

All the other cats looked at him like he had just crawled out from under a rock, but none of them dared to interrupt.

"I know that we're all cats, but in order to do things effectively, we're going to have to designate certain spots. I'll take the cul-de-sac since the people who adopted me then turned me loose live here. Guapo, you take the next section up."

"Right, boss," Guapo replied.

"Sassy, you take the far end of the street."

Sassy nodded but was concealing a scowl. She didn't like the far end of the street because that's where all the cars came and went. *He's probably making me do this because I'm the cutest,* she thought as she started swishing her tail.

"New Guy, you can be in the section between Sassy and Guapo."

New Guy nodded. Since he was a neighborhood feral and new to their little group, he didn't want to do anything to jeopardize his position.

Blue spoke again. "Before we go out and start on our duties, there are some important turf rules to go over.

"Rule #1: Don't start a fight with any other cat just because he or she is on your turf. I have just assigned you all your designated territories. Chaser will remain behind and supervise our progress."

Chaser frowned. Why did he have to stay behind? It's not like they couldn't have assigned him some territory in the subdivision next to theirs.

"I'm not staying behind while you enjoy all the action. What kind of half-baked plan is this, anyway?"

"Yeah," Sassy agreed. "Why shouldn't we be able to fight for our territories? No one should step his or her paws on my turf."

"I agree with Sassy," Fifi said. "We all know our own turf,

and here you go trying to change things. Besides, what if some outsider tries to come in and join our clowder? That would be completely unacceptable!"

"Enough!" Blue exclaimed after letting out a loud yowl. "Stop this inane bickering. I'm in charge here, and I picked the territories because it makes it easier than doing things completely willy nilly. In order to execute everything properly, we need organization! You can't just go butting heads and fighting over your own turf. It wouldn't look good in front of the humans.

"No other cats outside our clowder would dare to upset our plans. And if any of them are stupid enough to try, then dispose of them how you see fit. Those who have not been with us since the beginning have no right to encroach on our territory.

"Also, Anyone who dares to question again or defy my orders will be exiled from our little clowder. We have to work together if we want to gain the gullible humans' trust." Blue felt like he shouldn't have to explain that the territories he'd designated to them were merely part of a test to see if they could work well together.

After another moment of uncomfortable silence, Blue resumed explaining the rules.

"Rule #2: No attacking the humans. We need to lure them in with our natural cuteness and let them think that we're on their side."

"We *are* pretty irresistible," Sassy purred.

Blue chose to ignore her comment. He just assigned the three cats he trusted the most the duty of walking around the neighborhood meowing very loudly until at least one human opened his or her door. From there, they would let the humans adore them and bestow upon them many fine gifts. Blue really liked this plan, especially since he was a stray up until very recently. Why should he and his kind have to do everything themselves? Of course, all that would change as soon as they recruited some willing volunteers.

Most of the other cats meowed in agreement now that their plan was set, but Fifi was not satisfied. She didn't like humans, her owners most of all. Not only did they think it was funny to give her a name usually reserved for snooty French poodles, but they expected her to act the part as well.

"These humans are decimating the earth; they don't care about any life at all, not even theirs."

"Keep it to yourself, Fifi. This is not one of those green earth, clean earth, whatever protests. Just as long as we have a place to sleep and someone to feed us, then we'll be all right."

"But they're too stupid for their own good. If we were to get rid of them, we'd doing the world a great service."

"Not if no one's around to feed us!" Guapo said, fed up with all the sudden arguing.

Blue squinted. "I hadn't really thought of that."

"No, I guess you didn't!" Fifi hissed. She was getting really tired of his indecisiveness.

None of the clowder communicated anything for a few moments. Not being fed was a serious thing to ponder, and no cat ever wanted to think about something like that.

"So, you mean that there's no way we can take over the humans — not even using our natural charm?" New Guy finally asked after they had time to digest the dark thought. It seemed like all their planning would have to be delayed for a while, even if that meant lots of protesting later.

"Not without an army, like one not from this world." Fifi replied. "As I just said, humans are stupid. They can't even hear the words we try to say to them; everything comes out as meows."

"And we can't kill them because no one would be around to feed us." Sassy hesitated, looking over at the others, as if to gauge their thoughts. "What, do you think that the dogs could actually do it?"

The remark elicited laughter from the clowder. As if dogs would take care of cats; dogs can barely take care of themselves most of the time. The cats also knew that one good thing about getting rid of the humans would also mean getting rid of the dogs. But since that plan threatened their tummies and, ultimately, their existence, it could not be executed.

"Well, now what do we do?" an exasperated Blue asked, feeling like his entire life had just become devoid of purpose.

"We wait," Fifi replied. "Soon enough, those humans will realize that they need the help of a superior being. We cozy up to them like we want to be their friends, then give it more time." Fifi let out a little grin. "And, soon, we will have them exactly where we want them."

The rest of the clowder went silent again, and Blue shot Fifi a glance which seemed to indicate that he was never going to underestimate any of his kind again.

All continued to remain silent until the cats spied a car approaching the cul-de-sac. The unsuspecting human operating the vehicle couldn't help but think how cute all the cats looked sitting in the big circle toward the end of the street. She smiled and continued to head back home, where her husband was patiently waiting for her to return with their dinner.

Alley

*Purr*sonalities differ, even in cats.
No one could say that you are
Sweet or good-tempered;
Bite marks and scratches are
Evidence.
We could ask you many questions,
Such as, "Why do we keep you around?"
You are fed by our hands, yet you
Do not seem to do much for us.
There's no need to remove any
Rodent population, so your reflexes
And sharp claws are not needed here.

You beguile your sweet brother,
Who already knows that you are
The boss, and he only wants to feel
The kind of affection he gives,
Yet you offer him little comfort.

It seems that only the man of the house
Is worthy of your positive attention,
Something that goes back to your early kittenhood.
You were bottle fed by your previous owner's husband,
Whose milk easily fostered your love.

But what about the rest of us, whom you
So haughtily disregard?
And how do you know that we will love you
All the same?

Arrogance. It's the same kind which makes
Man believe that they are the only species worth anything.

Now we finally realize that there is not much
Difference between man and beast, so there's
Nothing else to do but continue in
Our roles, letting the rest of the world know
That hubris binds us together.

Elegante

I am beautiful;
My elegance has no
Way to be contained.
Look into my eyes,
Which resemble fine gems.
Eyes speak volumes,
Even though my vocabulary
Is limited.
And when I drink,
I do not merely lap;
My tongue dives ever so elegantly
Into the bowl.
Jumping to new heights
Is also a way to showcase
My limbs while envious
Humans watch my graceful
Muscles perform something
That theirs could never do.
My coat of many colors never
Ceases to amaze.
They like the touch and feel
Because it makes them calm.
When they get lost in my fur,
I revel in the fact that I have them
wrapped around my little paw.
Who knew that life could be so easy
When you are as beautiful
And graceful as I?

Sultry Velcro

So Much Love to Give

Jim and Angie had been married for over ten years, and some of their friends recently thought that they had been missing something in their lives.

They were a childfree couple, and they also owned no pets. That was about to change.

Tom and Abby had been their friends for a number of years — in fact, it was for almost all their lives. They knew what a loving couple Jim and Angie were — with so much more love than to give to two people alone; that's why they'd concocted this little surprise for them.

~*~

That evening, Jim was reading the paper, and Angie was working on a new painting. It was a landscape of their backyard, and she managed to capture the beautiful orange and purple of the landscape. She was quite pleased with the nearly finished result.

The doorbell rang, forcing them out of their thoughts and back into reality.

"I'll get it," Jim said, knowing that his wife was busy creating.

"Thanks," Angie replied while adding some finishing touches to the portion which she had just finished.

"Hello. Hello," Tom said as soon as Jim opened the door.

"Hi, Tom," Jim greeted his friend. "What brings you two out here tonight?" Jim acknowledged his friend's wife, Abby, who was still seated in the passenger seat of their car.

Abby reciprocated Jim's wave and unbuckled her seatbelt.

"I'll be out in a minute," Angela said, wiping her hands on her apron. In the foyer, she greeted the smiling face of her friend.

"Sorry I didn't come to the door earlier; I was working on one of my paintings. Where's Abby?"

"She's out getting something from the car."

Tom stepped into the house, as he heard Abby coming in after him.

Angela's eyes widened when she saw that Abby was lugging a pet carrier. That wasn't all; she also had a large dog in tow on a leash. From what Angela could see, it was a black Labrador.

Jim chuckled. "What, did you finally decide to let your kids have some more pets?" Tom and Abby got their kids a rabbit and a hamster. They felt they were still a little too young to take care of anything bigger than those.

"Nope. These are for you," Abby said, setting down the cat carrier and letting the huge beast of a dog walk into their house.

Tom let out a nervous laugh. "I don't think I heard you right, Abby. It sounded like you said that these animals were for us."

"They are," Tom replied, clapping him on the back. "They're an early anniversary gift for you guys."

Angie's smile faded to a bemused look in a matter of seconds. "You can't be serious. We don't know anything about pets." Her eyes darted over to the carrier. "What's in there?"

Abby went over to the carrier and opened the door. Out walked a beautiful white Persian. After surveying its surroundings, the cat minced to the middle of the room and lay down on the rug.

"Well, I guess that answers my question," Angie said to no one in particular.

"Don't worry," Tom said. "It's not that hard."

"Yeah," Abby interjected. "Feed them and make sure they have fresh water at all times. When they have to go to the bathroom, you let them outside. Well, you let the dog out, anyway."

Angela winced. "Are these things even potty trained?"

"Yes, the dog knows when to go to the door and scratch, and the cat has already been introduced to her litter box."

Well, that's a start, Angela thought as she placed her hands on her hips. Angela suspected that the gargantuan black Lab was a boy, but she couldn't be too sure.

"Which reminds me," Abby said right before heading back outside. "You're going to get the litter box and some food. You didn't think that we were going to start you off with nothing?"

"Well, thanks for thinking of us," Angela mumbled, not sure if anyone else heard.

Abby retrieved the litter box, which she carried in one hand. She held two nested bowls in the other.

"Let me just help her with this stuff, guys. I'll be right back. I'll leave you alone for a while so you can get acquainted."

Once both of them were out of the house, Jim and Angie looked over at the strange animals.

The cat was curled up in a little ball on the rug, and the dog just stared at them — his eyes seemed to ask, *what now?*

"Well, you've got to admit, they are kind of cute." Jim glanced at his wife, a little surprised. He knew that she wasn't really an animal person; he never really heard her refer to them as cute before.

"OK. I think that's it," Abby said once she and Tom had brought everything in and set it down.

"I'd recommend taking them to a vet soon. They've already been sterilized and had their shots. Here are the papers and certificates from the previous owners who rescued them." Tom said all this as he and Abby were getting ready to leave.

"If you need anything, just give us a call. Happy Anniversary, you guys!"

"Thank you," Jim and Angie said as they were trying to feign enthusiasm. They went over to the door to bid their friends goodnight, not knowing what to do once they were gone.

"That was weird," Jim said as soon as they were alone.

"You can say that again." Angie replied, feeling a little bit angry. "I mean, how can they just leave these animals here with us? What do they think we're going to do with them?"

"Well, they seem pretty confident that we're going to keep them as our pets. The people who rescued them clearly wanted to make sure that they were given a good home."

"Isn't there anyone we could give them to — put an ad in the paper?"

Jim put his hand on his chin, like he was pondering it. "Yeah, but that would probably make them mad. Can you imagine the looks on their faces when they come over to see us sans pets?"

Angie snickered. While she seemed amused by the whole idea, she also knew that Jim was right.

"Yeah, I can't argue with you there, but what are we going to do with a cat and dog?"

Jim couldn't help but feel a little sorry for Angie. He knew that she'd never had much exposure to animals. He had at least had a dog when he was a child. His name was Barky. Jim looked over at the black Lab, hoping that he would not keep up that tradition.

"Tell you what," he said to his wife, who still wore the same bemused expression on her face. "I'll go ahead and set some food out for the dog, and you can see if the cat's hungry."

"How will I know that?" Angela indicated the cat, who was now sleeping peacefully the floor.

"The best way to find out is to open a bag of food and put it out in front of her."

Angela shrugged and followed her husband over to the food.

As soon as the bags were opened and some of the contents poured out into the bowls, both the dog and the cat looked over in their direction. The kitty was quick to get on her paws and run over to her bowl, but the dog had already beaten her and was beginning to eat from his bowl.

"I guess I should get them some water to wash it all down."

"Good idea, and while you're doing that, I can set up the litter box. All you do is pour the mix into the box, right?" Angela felt a little dumb asking that question, but she wanted to make sure she was doing things correctly.

"That sounds like as good an idea as any," Jim said as he watched the dog move over from the food bowl to the water.

The cat was still in the middle of her meal.

After the animals finished eating, they went to the center of the rug to lie down together.

Jim came over and put his arm around Angela. They couldn't help but think how cute it was to see the animals snuggled up like they were.

"Isn't that sweet?" Angela said, gesturing toward the animals.

Jim couldn't help but notice that his wife was taking to them. If she decided to keep the dog and cat as pets, that would be all right with him — just as long as Angie was happy and comfortable with the situation.

"You know what, Jim?"

"What's that?" he replied, kissing her on the temple.

"I think that we should go to bed right now so that this image will stay in our minds as we sleep."

Jim chuckled.

"Sure. Why not? And when we wake up tomorrow, we might discover that this was only a dream."

That two of them went to bed, enjoying the peaceful tranquility which sleep had brought them.

~*~

A few hours later, they awoke to some thumping outside their door. The thumping was followed by meows.

Angie looked over at their alarm clock sitting on the nightstand.

"You've got to be kidding me!" she mumbled, discovering that it was only 6:15 a.m. on a Saturday. That cat had some nerve waking her at this time in the morning!

It must be time for her royal highness's morning feeding. Angie quietly rose from their bed and tiptoed over to the door. As soon as she cracked it open, the cat tried to poke herself inside.

"Oh, no you don't." Angie hissed, afraid that the cat would come in and wake up Jim. Angie gently pushed her out the door and led her to her bowl. The dog barked. She told him to be quiet. He obeyed, a little to her surprise.

"Oh, no!" Jim heard her exclaim. He leaped out of bed to see what was the matter.

"Honey, what's wrong?"

"I'll tell you what's wrong, this *thing* is peeing all over the rug! I thought it was housebroken."

Jim immediately went to the door, opened it, and led the dog outside. He quickly closed it behind him.

"What happened to last night?" Angela huffed. "They were looking all cute when they cuddled together, and now this is going on!" She went into the kitchen and returned with her multi-purpose vacuum and some carpet cleaner.

"We're calling Tom and to come and take their *gifts* back! They can't expect me to take this anymore!" Angela said all this as she was cleaning the carpet. "This is worse than having a kid!"

Jim went over to Angie just as she was finished vacuuming up all the liquid.

"I wouldn't say that, but pets do require more care. Since you're not used to animals, I could do most of the work — at least with the dog."

"I hate to ask that much of you, but I would really appreciate it. Maybe you can give me some pointers."

"I'll do the best I can," Jim replied. "But, there is one thing we should probably do soon."

"What's that?"

"Give them names."

~*~

Two weeks had passed, and things seemed to be going much more smoothly. Angela had bonded with both animals. She was helping Jim more with the basic care, and she even started playing with them.

They'd named both animals. Angie decided to name the cat Snowflake because she was a fluffy, white ball.

Jim thought that was cute, but he wanted to name the dog. He decided to call him Shadow because it sounded cool. Also, it was because he followed them around the house.

Surprisingly, the dog and cat did not fight much. They almost acted like litter mates, as they played and even ate together.

Jim and Angie were both relieved that they were settling into a routine. This would not last very long, however, because things were going to change soon.

Shadow started barking madly at the front door. He'd already gone a few minutes ago, so he didn't need to go out for that.

"What are you doing there, Shadow, hmm?" Jim patted the panting dog on the head.

Shadow let out another bark before Jim eyed the door suspiciously.

He wasn't quite sure what was out there, but he didn't think he wanted to know anymore. Jim opened the door to another cat and dog sitting on the front porch. They seemed to be strays because they weren't wearing collars.

Angie was at the store, so she wasn't home to witness his letting them come into the kitchen for some food and water.

Shadow and Snowball didn't mind these strange animals coming into *their* home. In fact, they seemed intrigued by their presence. The established pets followed them into the kitchen, perhaps in hopes of getting something more to eat.

Jim laughed as he opened up another bag of both dog and cat food. He also set out some new bowls for their visitors. Jim watched the four of them chow down, wondering how long it had been since the strays had anything to eat or drink. It was really quite amusing how their old pets paid such attention to the tabby cat and the yellow Lab.

After the new animals were fed, Jim led them back to the front door and urged them back outside. They seemed a little reluctant to leave. Shadow and Snowball didn't want them to go, either.

"What is with you guys, huh?" Jim asked as soon as he closed the door. He was kind of relieved to see that the pets stopped making noise and that Angie wasn't home to witness this.

Shadow and Snowball went over to the window to see the runaways still standing outside on the porch. He thought that he should go outside and shoo them away, but he also couldn't help but think how cute it was that they were starting to make friends.

Jim moved away from the window and heard Angela's car pull into the driveway moments later. This had scared the other cat and dog away, as they were gone by the time Angela came to the door — arms filled with grocery bags. Jim opened the door for her then went outside to help her retrieve the rest.

"Hey, hon." Angela kissed Jim. They both went into the kitchen to put away the groceries. "What would you like me to make you for dinner tonight?"

"Actually, I was just thinking about ordering a pizza. Let's take a little time out for us."

Angela smiled; she liked the sound of that. Since these two had come into their lives, they'd had a little less downtime. A movie sounded nice right after the walks and feedings and attention. Jim dialed the pizza place, wondering if their little friends had come back.

"I'll get it," Jim said when the doorbell rang.

"Here you go," the kid said. "That'll be sixteen bucks."

Jim handed him the $20.00 and told him to keep the change.

"Thanks, man. Hey, by the way, this cat and dog out here really want to get into your house. One of them kept rubbing up against my legs — getting a little too friendly, if you know what I mean."

Jim couldn't say that he was surprised to see the vagabonds had returned. He sighed and told the kid it was OK to let them in. The guy thanked Jim and went back to his car.

He really didn't want to have to deal with this tonight, and he knew that Angie wouldn't want to, either. So much for a quiet night with a pizza and movie!

Jim brought the pizza into the living room. Just as he feared, Angela saw the cat and dog follow him.

"What's this? Do our pets have friends over for dinner?"

Jim could tell that Angela was nervous and skeptical, even though she tried to hide behind her sense of humor. He set the pizza down on the table, wondering if she had lost her appetite.

"Well, I have a confession to make; these animals came around this afternoon while you were gone. I gave them some food and water. It also seems that our pets have gotten attached to them."

As Jim was telling her this, she just looked at him like she was questioning his sanity. She studied his face for a while to see if he was ready to burst out laughing. He didn't change the guilty expression on his face.

Neither she nor Jim knew anything about the strays other than the fact that they showed up on their property, so they decided to take them out to the garage and feed them again in there. All it took was for Jim to rattle the bag, and they followed him to the desired destination. He did not want to ruin the quiet night that he had promised his wife.

The next morning, they opted to take the two strays to the vet Abby and Tom had recommended. It was a laborious task getting them into the car; both the cat and dog vocalized their protest. They were hoping that the vet could recommend a no kill shelter or another patient who would like a dog and/or cat.

The couple made their way up to the window and announced that they were there for their appointment.

The vet told Angie that her suspicions were correct. The stray tabby was a male, and the golden retriever was a female.

They thanked the vet and asked him about finding a good home for the strays.

~*~

The following afternoon, the couple inquired about adoptive prospects for the stray dog and cat. The vet asked if they had any interest in keeping them, since their other two were attached to them.

Jim and Angie's eyes widened; of course they hadn't thought about it. They were too busy trying to take care of the two that they already had.

"I'll just go out in the hall and give you a moment to talk this over privately."

As soon as he left the room, Jim and Angie just looked at each other for a second, silently, like they were forming arguments, both for and against keeping the strays.

"You wanna give it a try? I mean, we've already had these two for a while. What could two more hurt?"

Angela smiled, and all Jim had to do was see that smile on her face to know that she was willing to give it a go.

"What can I say, I'm an animal person."

Jim reached over and hugged Angie. Though he would not have admitted it before, he wouldn't mind having another pair of pets to love. The furry portion of their family was soon to be complete.

The vet was happy to hear the news and asked them if they had come up with any names yet. Jim told him they would have to get back to him on that. It would be one of their first tasks as soon as they got back home.

~*~

A few days passed, and Jim and Angie now felt fulfilled. They decided to name the golden Lab Sunny and the tabby cat Stripes. Not very original, but they were cute and enough to make them feel satisfied with their new family.

While Jim and Angie joked around with each other about the cumbersome task of caring for four pets, they felt the great bond between man and animal.

What helped matters was the fact that each animal had their own sweet and loveable personalities. Like most pets, they had their annoying traits too, but that didn't make Jim and Angie love them any less.

When they told Tom and Abby that they had adopted two other pets, their friends were both surprised and delighted.

They said that they would have to make it a point to come over soon and meet their new friends.

Jim and Angie were still able to enjoy their quiet evenings together. They also got to enjoy nights on town because the pets had adjusted to their new surroundings and didn't get into what they weren't supposed to — most of the time.

Two months earlier, neither Jim nor Angie knew that such a thing was possible, but now they couldn't imagine life without their four adorable fur-babies: Snowball, Shadow, Sunny, and Stripes.

Since these great additions came into their lives, the couple changed a lot. They became aware of issues affecting animals worldwide and made charitable contributions to help prevent cruelty against animals.

As recently as one month ago, Jim and Angie never would have thought that their lives would yield such a great change. The couple had been completely happy with their family of two, but after some intervention from their friends and fate, they realized that the adoption of their four fur babies allowed them to grow even closer to each other.

Boudicca in Her Majesty's Cabinet

Here Kitty, Kitty

Your little paws come
Racing down the street
Every time I call your name.
We are eager to be reunited
After mere hours of your absence.

Just like you,
I had many
Things to do.

While I poured over the words
Of my next book, you went
Hunting for a cat-sized feast,
Or adventure.

Our dinnertime draws near,
But I can't feed myself
Until I feed you;
Your bossy meow demands it!

The evenings are our time
Together.
You've done all you wanted—
As much as
Your little paws can take.

I am also through with my
Daily tasks,
Having taxed
My brain.

You think that I should be honored
To bask in your company this evening,
And you're right.

The pleasure has been all mine.
Never a greater companion
I could find to share my bed
And talk to about my day.

We lay ourselves
Down to sleep,
Your little head
On the pillow next to mine.
This must be
What heaven feels like.
I am truly blessed!

Ragged Concern

A few years ago, our homeowners' association sent out a newsletter concerning feral cats in the neighborhood. They started by thanking us for our kindness in providing the cats food and water.

They also said that they were becoming somewhat of a problem, suggesting that there are many roaming around our subdivision. I, personally, do not consider them a nuisance. In fact, it brightens my day when one (or more) come(s) to visit. Yes, I am aware that there are certain individuals who do not like cats. I'm also aware of the dangers concerning overpopulation. And it brings to mind those public announcements from Bob *Barker* urging us to spay and neuter our pets. (Ironically, the newsletter mentioned nothing about feral dogs.)

At first, I thought those on the homeowner's board were only concerned with the aesthetics of our properties, but then I read the part about their volunteering to take the cats to shelters and paying to have them sterilized. I couldn't help but admire their kindness in wanting to protect the quality of life of those dear strays, who many of us welcome into our neighborhood with open hearts.

Office Assistant Taylor

Herding Cats

Gathering such a
Wild assortment is
Far from easy,
Especially when one
Considers all the
Hurdles of daily life.

Though times have been
Established, other
Elements often go
Against the clock.
Whether by force
Or choice, it does
Not really matter;
Our absences always
Leave a void.

Getting certain parties
Together is like
Herding cats, I'm often told,
And we are our own clowder.
Those outside looking in,
Though not ignorant
Of our plight,
Could never know all
The complexities involved
In trying to come together.
Only when others realize
The importance of our

Gatherings will they see
The light in knowing what
We are trying to do — write!

*previously published in *Herding Cats and Other Alien Creatures: The Indian Creek Anthology Series Volume 21*

Jungle Cats

Jungle cats never lose
Their playful nature;
Most of us are just
Too afraid to see it.

Human eyes signal fear
To our brains because
We are not on top of
The food chain.

Show me a lion
Or a tiger that doesn't
Want to sit in a box
Or bat things with their paws,
Then you may call me a liar…

…After you've had the courage
To stay and witness it for yourself!

About the Author

Jen Selinsky was born in Pittsburgh, PA. In 2003, she earned her bachelor's degree in English from Clarion University of Pennsylvania. In 2004, she earned her master's degree in library science from the same school. Jen has worked as a professional librarian for over twelve years. She has published more than 180 books. Her work can be found on <u>Lulu</u>, <u>Amazon</u>, <u>Barnes & Noble</u>, <u>Kobo</u>, <u>iTunes</u>, <u>Smashwords</u>, <u>Pen It!</u> <u>Publications</u>, and <u>Books-A-Million</u>, as well as many others. She has also been featured in publications such as: *The Courier Journal*, *The News and Tribune*, *Explorer* Magazine, *Liphar* Magazine, and *Indiana Libraries*. Jen lives in Sellersburg, IN with her husband.

www.ingramcontent.com/pod-product-compliance
Lightning Source LLC
Chambersburg PA
CBHW061451170626
46811CB00004B/1454